Cows Can't Fly

For Bill
and
Steve

Cows can't Fly

Written and Illustrated by David Milgrim

PUFFIN BOOKS

Cows can't fly,
but I don't care.
One day I drew
some in the air!

"Why, that's absurd," my father said. "Why don't you draw some birds instead?"

But then, like magic,
came a breeze
that grabbed my cows
and shook the trees.

And in a breath,
before my eyes,
my flying cows
were flying high!

My drawing flew off
far away,
but where it went
I cannot say. . . .

Next thing I knew,
to my surprise,
a flock of cattle
fluttered by!

They flapped and flew
and filled the sky,
quite unaware
that cows can't fly.

"I'd love to see
a flying cow,"
my mother said,
"but not just now."

My grandma said,
"If cows can fly,
then why, pray tell,
can't you and I?"

You don't see **me** flying, do you?

And everyone
I told downtown
was much too busy
looking down.

So no one saw
the cows but me,
but what a sight
they were to see!

Because if cows
can soar the sky,
who knows what else
might start to fly. . . .

PUFFIN BOOKS
Published by the Penguin Group
Penguin Putnam Books for Young Readers, 345 Hudson Street, New York, New York 10014, U.S.A.
Penguin Books Ltd, 27 Wrights Lane, London W8 5TZ, England
Penguin Books Australia Ltd, Ringwood, Victoria, Australia
Penguin Books Canada Ltd, 10 Alcorn Avenue, Toronto, Ontario, Canada M4V 3B2
Penguin Books (N.Z.) Ltd, 182-190 Wairau Road, Auckland 10, New Zealand

Penguin Books Ltd, Registered Offices: Harmondsworth, Middlesex, England

First published in the United States of America by Viking, a member of Penguin Putnam, Inc., 1998
Published by Puffin Books, a member of Penguin Putnam Books for Young Readers, 2000

1 3 5 7 9 10 8 6 4 2

Copyright © David Milgrim, 1998
All rights reserved

THE LIBRARY OF CONGRESS HAS CATALOGED THE VIKING EDITION AS FOLLOWS:
Milgrim, David.
Cows can't fly / by David Milgrim.
p. cm.
Summary: After drawing a picture of cows that is blown away by a breeze,
a child tries to convince others that cows are flying through the air.
(1. Imagination—Fiction. 2. Cows—Fiction. 3. Stories in rhyme.)
I. Title. PZ8.3.M5776Co (E)—dc21 1998 97-25434 CIP AC

Puffin Books ISBN 0-14-056721-6

Printed in the United States of America
Set in Avant Garde